Ela's Diary

Vivian Olson

PUBLISHED BY

SIGMA'S
BOOKSHELF

MINNETONKA, MN 55305
WWW.SIGMASBOOKSHELF.COM

Chapter 1

Mom

It was 2:00 a.m. and my clock was beeping. Another busy day in Hoffoloff. I swung my legs out of bed and started my day with a little breakfast of eggs and toast before getting dressed for work. I had a nagging feeling that something wasn't quite right.

Suddenly my phone rang in its annoying "ring, ring song" that I can't seem to change. I answered and found Tanya, my best friend, on the other end.

"I was going out to get my mail when I saw my next door neighbor, you know, your mom, walk out of her house," she said, practically panting. "She walked across the street, opened her mailbox, took out her mail, then got halfway across the street and was hit by a car. The car stopped when the driver realized what had happened. I think your mom is okay, but I'm not sure."

I dropped the phone, flopped on my bed and began to cry. I looked at my clock and it was 2:30 in the morning. By this time, everyone on the tiny island should be awake, except for the newborn to three-year-olds, who wake up at 3:00 a.m.

I'm not sure how long I was lying there, but as soon as

I found my strength and built up some courage, I picked up my phone, which I had carelessly dropped onto my bed, pushed down the receiver to get back a dial tone, then called my boss to tell her I wouldn't be at work today.

The phone rang three times before Katy answered. "Hi, this is Katy. Who am I speaking to?"

"Hi, this is Ela. I won't be able to come to work today. I hope you understand." With that I hung up, not giving her much of an explanation, and dropped the phone on my bed before getting dressed to go and visit my mom.

I got in my car and drove two miles to the only hospital on our island. When I arrived at the hospital I looked up and saw the big red letters that spell out "St. Harold Hoffoloff Hospital." I attempted to walk into the large, bleak, white building; but right as the automatic doors slid open, a woman with white hair blocked my way.

"What is your business here?" she asked in an unfamiliar accent. She looked familiar, but I couldn't put my finger on where I had seen her before.

I was genuinely surprised. I had been to the hospital many times before, sadly, and never had I been stopped like this before. As I opened my mouth to answer, a woman wearing a knee length, bright red dress came over. She spoke calmly to the woman who blocked my way.

"Come on. You are supposed to be asleep, not stopping people from entering the hospital!" She gave a fake giggle as she led the woman away from the door and down a hallway.

I really hate people who can't get ahold of their emotions, or sound like they just inhaled helium. So, that woman who unblocked my way really *got to me.*

Anyway…I walked to the front desk, my shoes squeaking on the hard floors.

"Can you tell me what room my mother, Alberta Rose, is in?" I asked. She must have thought I was in the wrong place because she pointed at the door to the pet store! I know I'm short, but really!?

"Ugh, no, I am here to see my mom, Alberta Rose," I responded slowly, becoming more and more annoyed. People who work at this hospital never have been very hospitable.

She looked slowly at her computer, her cheeks becoming red. "Well, um, yes! She is in room 72, which is down the hall." She didn't even look up when I thanked her, but I could see that her whole face was red.

I walked down the hall looking at the room numbers. 10… 25… 50… 65…70… 72! When I reached that room, I knocked on the closed wooden door. The lady I had seen wearing the bright red dress opened the door. As she did so, a barn owl flew out of the room and landed on my head. I was freaking out inside, but I didn't move, not one inch.

"Don't worry! She's harmless!" Her voice cracked from "speaking" too high. She reached towards the bird, but as she did so the bird's talons dug into my scalp, then everything went pitch black.

Chapter 2

Coming Home

The wind howled in my ears, the night sky turning blacker than I thought possible. Any comfort of home was gone, and one lonely barn owl hooted as it flew off to hunt.

I opened my eyes, my heart pounding with fear. "Where am I?" I asked.

I appeared to be in a white room with a chair, a television, and a nightstand with an electric clock on top of it. It was cold in that room, and had a feeling of loneliness and sorrow. A door opened and a woman walked in. When she saw I was awake, she rushed over to me and pushed on my shoulders to lay me down.

"What am I doing here?" I asked, wonder boiling up in me.

"Well, when that owl landed on your head and dug its talons into your scalp..." I reached up to where the bird had landed and felt the faint marks it left behind. Wait! Why was there an owl in a hospital? "It hit a nerve that caused you to, um..."

I burst out before she could say any more. "Well, would you just get to the point?!?"

"I beg your pardon! What did you just say?"

"I said..." Just then the door swung open and my dad and 12-year-old little sister rushed in.

"Oh, my, gosh!!! What happened to your face?" Angela asked.

"Um, nothing that I know of?" I answered as I touched my face.

"Then why are your eyes all weird?" She was getting sassy now, like she owned the world and it didn't matter what she said. She was obviously enjoying knowing something that I didn't.

"Angela!" my father scolded.

"What?" she asked.

I tried to ask more, but I fell into a sort of sleep first. For a while, most things were a little bit blurry. I slowly returned to full consciousness to the smell of roses filling the room. I opened my eyes to see a thousand roses stuck in my face. Actually, only twelve, but still the thorns really hurt!

"Hi Ela, how are you?" Jack asked as he withdrew the flowers from my face and placed them in a vase on the nightstand next to the bed.

"Well, obviously I've been better, but I think I'm fine."

"Ela Darling," the nurse said, "do you want to see a mirror so you can see what your sister was talking about before you dozed off?" She gave me a hand mirror with a green and gold twisting border around it.

"Ahh!!!" I screamed.

If you are so inclined to wonder why I screamed, it was because of the appearance of my face.

"What's wrong, Ela Darling?" Angie teased.

"Angie, stop."

"Why, *Ela Darling*?" she asked, making a silly and stupid face, directed at me.

"Because I told you to!!" I screamed. The words felt foreign in my mouth and reminded me of how my mom dealt with Angie. The room went quiet as I took in my appearance.

I was almost unrecognizable. My usually fiery red hair

was now snow white. My usually blue eyes were entirely dark turquoise. My eyebrows were now black, and my nose, oh my nose, my nose was flat! But that isn't even the worst part. How my mouth looked was worse. I only had a top lip. No lip coloring or skin that would make my mouth look whole, just my teeth. It really was a horrific sight.

"Ela..." Jack began.

"What!" I yelled as loud as I could. My face felt hot now, a little *too* hot.

"Ela, cool down. Get some rest. We will leave you alone for a little while. We'll all come back a little before lunch," Jack continued, trying to calm me down.

I glanced at the clock. It was 5:00 a.m. My head felt heavy and well-worn as I laid it back on my uncomfortable hospital pillow and closed my 23-year-old eyes. I drifted off into a land of ice. I was in a dress that made me look like I was at a party in Hawaii. I walked around only to find ice and more ice. I continued walking, turning four times before realizing I was in a box, a cardboard one it seemed.

"Help!" I called out, my voice echoing in the empty silence. After that I woke up. I kept my eyes closed because the effort of opening them was too much at the time.

"What happened to her face?" my best friend Tanya asked, thinking I was still asleep.

"Hopefully she wakes up soon. Her lunch is here and it's gonna get eaten by either me or her," Jack sighed. I could feel his weight rest on the end of my bed.

I opened my eyes to acknowledge that I was awake. "Hi!" I spoke to no one in particular, a yawn interrupting.

"Good afternoon Ela Darling. Good to see you up!" the nurse exclaimed, excited about something that I didn't understand.

"Elizabeth?" My dad said questioningly. I knew he was serious because he used my full name. No one ever did that.

"What?" I yawned.

"I have something to tell you. Um, Tanya, do you want to tell her?"

He looked over at Tanya who sighed and rolled her eyes and then began, "Ela, your mom is home! She left last night, well and fine!" She looked so happy, but something reared up inside of me wanting to wipe that smile off of her face.

"WHAT!!" I yelled. My voice must have been louder than I thought because everyone looked at me surprised.

Chapter 3

Paralysis

"I thought you would be excited..." Tanya mumbled, looking at me, but avoiding my eyes.

"Are you kidding me? You thought that I would be excited? Well you thought wrong! The whole reason I am in this stupid hospital is because I came to visit my mom! If she isn't here, then why am I? Don't get me wrong. I am glad she is still alive, but I would like to leave! Why can't I leave?" I was steaming, clenching my fists under the sheets.

"Well..." Tanya began, but she turned away before she could finish, fidgeting with her fingers.

"Well what?!" I was getting impatient now. No one seemed to tell me anything straight up anymore. Everyone wanted to hide behind another person!

"Well... we have some more news for you," Jack burst in. It was quite clear he didn't want to have to be the one to tell me whatever it was as he stopped and looked over at Tanya.

"More?" I tried to shout. It was supposed to come out as a scream, but it was barely a whisper.

"Well... well, you're..." Jack paused, seemingly at a loss for words. He opened his mouth to speak, but it was Tanya who did.

"Well, you're paralyzed!" she blurted out.

"Are you joking? This has to be a joke!" I knew something was terribly wrong, but I didn't guess that it was paralysis. My eyes filled up with tears as I glanced down at the mirror still on my chest. It was a scary sight to see. Tears were falling from my bloodshot eyes and onto my warm cheeks.

"It's going to be okay Ela," Jack comforted as he pulled the hair out of my face.

"Ugh! Why does everyone say that? Because it won't be! Nothing will be okay because I will be stuck in this stupid hospital for who knows how long! Could someone please scratch the bottom of my foot?" I asked.

"Why can't you do it?" Angela asked, looking at me like I was the one who wasn't smart.

"Because... I'm... I'm, paralyzed." My voice hurt as I spat out the words. They seemed so weird, almost foreign on my tongue. I looked at the clock again. It was 7:30 a.m. and I could smell the hospital food on the nightstand next to me. "That food looks good. Could someone feed me please? I'm famished!"

Suddenly without warning my eyelids closed and I was back in the ice box. Since I had nothing better to do, not to mention I was starving, I walked along the border of the box looking for a door. I didn't think there was one as I didn't notice one before, but I wanted to try. It would take me a while to walk around it because I couldn't see the other side of the box from where I stood. As I went on I became colder and colder. I felt like I was a brick of ice, but I continued on. The ground started to shake and ice fell. I tried to move out of the way, but I was so cold I could not move. I yelled out for help, but no one was there. As a block of ice fell on me from the roof of the box, I woke up.

My family and friends were surrounding me. I tried to speak, but my lip went numb, my head felt cold and my arms went limp as I spoke my last real word, "Help!"

Chapter 4

Realization

The next thing I know I am surrounded by the people who mean the most to me: Angela, Dad, Piper Emixer, Jack, Memna, and Allie. The only ones missing are my mom, Aunt Sophie, and my brother Kris. Then I notice someone in the corner that no one is acknowledging. He is in all black clothing, including a cape. It is an interesting outfit, but before I can ask anyone who that person is, he moves closer to the door and vanishes. No one is talking to me, but they are talking to each other like it's a big family reunion.

I tried to roll over to talk to Angie, who was on my left talking to Jack, but wait, I couldn't move! I tried to turn my head to face Angie, but even that simple task was impossible. The only things that moved were my aching arms.

I had an idea. I would use my arms to push myself onto my side so I could face her. I was too tired to do anything though. I had a little panic attack in my head because of my lack of movement. My arms moved in every direction. I had completely lost control of them. If only I could break this impenetrable shell of paralysis! I figured if I could get a pen or even a pencil and a piece of paper, I could write out the many questions running through my head.

I tried to grasp a nearby pen that had been abandoned on my bed, but it slipped out of my hand. I tried again and succeeded. About half of the people in the room were now looking at me. I used my right arm to grasp a piece of paper on the nightstand. I scratched out a couple of words, then dropped the pen. I stretched out my left hand before grabbing the pen again. Now the entire room was looking at me, including the nurse who was still smiling. A puzzled look washed over the crowd as my mind went berserk! Can't anyone understand me! Can anyone tell time? I can! I'm 23. I can read, write, ride a bike, drive a car, and so much more, but more importantly, I can tell time!

Chapter 5

More Important Things

My anger and frustration was boiling up in me as the attention of the group fixed itself back on a wooden box at the foot of my bed. I wanted so badly to move, but as I have stated before, I couldn't. I was trapped in my own mind. Thoughts pounding against the walls of my head, trying to break free. No one to talk to, as no sound would come from of my mouth.

While everyone still talked and laughed like I wasn't there, I fell asleep. I drifted off to the ice box where I was curled up on the cardboard ground. I could feel a nonexistent sun on my back as the ice block that had fallen on me in the previous dream began to melt off of me. I became much warmer, but also drenched in ice water.

I looked to the ground to see a shivering and wet tiny bunny. Its fur was flattened from the water and it was like holding ice when I scooped up the little fur ball. I walked a little ways towards the center of the box, tripping over my own feet, then I woke up.

It was just my mom, dad and sister in the room. I hadn't seen them all in the same room together in nine years.

"Well, I am glad her face is healing," my mom said in a faraway voice like I wasn't really there.

"Yeah, but I like her better when she can't move or talk!" Angela exclaimed, a smile spreading across her face.

"Angie!" The words had escaped my mouth before I knew what had happened.

"She, she talked! Um, sorry?" Angela said, rubbing her head nervously, noticing I was awake.

My parents looked towards the door, obviously looking for the nurse. I had something to say, but no one was looking at me. I flailed my arms like a beached dolphin trying to wave over their attention, but my mouth couldn't form another word or noise.

In the process of waving my arms, I managed to knock the electric clock off of the nightstand. It crashed onto the floor and smashed into a thousand pieces. That sure grabbed their attention as they looked to me and then the clock on the floor. As my parents looked at the clock, their eyes went blank. I didn't know it, but my life was soon going to get more complicated and weird.

Chapter 6

Great Grandma Melissa

I pulled my arms up to motion, "What?" so I could understand why my parents were so freaked out about a clock.

"That was your Great Grandma Melissa's clock, my grandmother. It was the only thing we had of hers. I know it seems sort of silly to hold onto a clock, but it was just something we had of hers." My dad's face fell when he really soaked in what had just happened.

"Great Grandma Melissa had a great granddaughter who wasn't adopted like the rest of the family. She is someone you may know. Piper Emixer is her name," my mom said, wringing her hands and looking a bit nervous.

My mind seemed to go a million miles an hour, trying to grasp the concept that Piper, my old friend, is somehow related to me and my parents never told me! Does Angie know? Does Piper know? Why wasn't I told sooner? How exactly are we related? Second cousins? Third cousins? Is she somehow my aunt? Why am I freaking out over this? I wanted to ask, but my voice was lost and I soon fell asleep.

I was back in the ice box, but the ice was melting now and water was dripping from the "ceiling?" It was bright and there was some source of light resembling a sun, but I couldn't see where it was coming from.

My mind kept wandering as I wandered, still holding the little bunny. I thought about what my parents had told me about Piper while I was awake. I really wasn't watching where I was going because I walked into a tree made out of cardboard, (ironic) and a door swung open. Deciding whether I should go through the door was surprisingly hard, so I slept on it, literally. I slept in the tree. When I closed my eyes within the dream, I floated back into reality.

Chapter 7

Memories of Things that Never Happened

When I opened my eyes I didn't see the blank white hospital room, but a very familiar greenish blue room. I noticed Angela sitting in a rocking chair in the corner of the room, absentmindedly rocking herself and reading something. I looked to the other side of the room at my mom, who was sorting out a box of something that looked like junk. Then I noticed my dad pacing back and forth in front of my bed, lines etched in his face as he looked down, evidently worried.

When he saw I was awake he exclaimed in great excitement, "Ela! She's awake! Alberta, Angela! Come here!" Angie and my mom ran over to me and started talking rapidly at the same time saying,

"Wow, wow, wow! I, I mean we are so happy. We were so worried! You were asleep for two days!!"

A breeze filled the room. Not an ordinary one, but one like the night before a hurricane gets worse. I had a feeling that I wasn't really in my childhood home. I wanted something, something so strong it was not real, something like

Lillly. I know it should be spelled L-i-l-y, or L-i-l-l-y, but I am talking about Lillly M. Trinity.

I looked around to see if I could spot her. I noticed I was not paralyzed anymore, so I stood up and walked around towards where Angela had been sitting. I saw what she had been reading. It was my old diary! I was so mad I kicked over the chair and found a secret door. That breeze pushed me in and I felt like I was falling, but something wasn't right about it.

I heard five voices. I recognized four of them, Mom, Dad, Angela, and Kris! Yet the fifth voice was a mystery. As the voices became louder it became brighter. After what seemed to be thirty seconds of falling, I hit the ground only to find out that the fifth voice belonged to Lillly.

"Kris!" I shouted when I regained my strength after the fall.

"Elly!" he responded. "Oh, when was the last time I saw my favorite sister?" He looked at me as he gave me a hug before realizing Angie was in the room too. She gave him a large snarl and turned away.

"I haven't seen you since Aunt Sophie took you to, Mine-ern-a-so-tsa?" I stuttered. I soon found out it is pronounced Minnesota (what a weird name…). "Mom, dad, what is going on? Where am I? Who are those people up there?" I asked.

"Well, when you fell asleep a girl walked in and said she knew you or rather wrote that she knew you and that she could bring you back to your normal self. Of course we agreed, but…" Angie stopped there and took a deep breath, then she fainted.

"Angie! What just happened? She does know I was talking to really anyone but her? And what was the girl's name?" I continued to ask. Nothing was making sense anymore. I wish it could all go back to how it was!

"Ela, would you like me to continue where Angela left off?" my mom asked.

"Oh, I would love it if you would tell me the name of the girl!"

"Ah, what was her name? I think it was something like Lillly Michelle Trinity? Something like that."

"Mom! Why do you hate me?!" I screeched. Then I tried to climb up the hole I had fallen into, to try and get away from my mom and especially Lillly.

I then realized that Kris and Angela (who was unconscious on the floor that was made of dirt) had no idea who, or more specifically what, Lillly is. I started to explain. "Lillly is a 2,214-year-old teenager. She is always trying to help people in the hospital, but whenever she uses her magic, everything goes wrong. Even though I am fine I will go back to when I was in the hospital, paralyzed."

I paused and began to silently cry. I thought if I am fine now, I should enjoy it while it lasts. "How do we get out of here?" I asked, trying to discreetly wipe the tears from my eyes.

This time Lillly spoke. "Turtles are purple. Unicorns are green. I really hate people who are mean!"

"She has been talking like that all day and we can't figure out..."

"Oranges are green. Apples are orange. I really, really hate people who are mean!!" Lillly interrupted.

Angela sat up and yawned before screeching, "Shut your mouth!!"

"I cartwheeled a locker. I ate a TV, and now my monkey needs to eat!"

"I said to shut your MOUTH!! We are trying to think!" Angela yelled. The room seemed to vibrate with the ferocity of her voice.

"I think I know what she is saying," I interjected as the ground started to shake.

"Well tell us!" My brother was hardly ever mad, so how he raised his voice and clenched his fists worried me.

"I-I only know what s-she's saying because I went to camp with her 12 years ago. I might be a little rusty. Well, she's saying…"

All of a sudden before anyone could say anything more, the room began to spin and I realized I had fallen up somehow and that is why it felt so weird. We were now falling at a very fast speed. Then the room became so quiet, it didn't seem real. Just as the knot in my stomach grew to be too much, the lights went out.

Chapter 8

Princess and the Pea

I opened my eyes to see nothing upon nothing upon nothing. It seemed as though the darkness would never end. I stood up on something squishy. It felt a bit like a damp sponge, only it wasn't wet. I stood up and I hit my head on the ceiling and fell backwards onto the sponge-like thing. I tried again, but I figured it might be smart to crawl instead. I slowly moved forward and I ended up falling off of a mega-tall thing.

I hit the ground and a light flickered on. I jumped up, completely unharmed and looked to the thing I had fallen from. It was a bed that was sagging under the weight of what appeared to be 40 mattresses and one blanket, all stacked on top of each other.

What was amazing was that I couldn't feel any broken bones or see any bruises, but I also couldn't see the ceiling.

"Mother! Mother! Come quick! She's awake! Yes, she really is! No, I am not lying again!" a male voice called from nearby.

"Well, tell her the good news if she really is up!" a female voice screamed through a door on the other side of the room.

"Ugh! Mother, you never believe me!" the male voice called again.

The owner of the voice slowly came walking into the room and he looked like an 18-year-old spoiled rotten prince! "So, how'd yah sleep?" he asked, looking quite annoyed.

"Actually, I didn't sleep," I replied. I was going to continue, but the prince's face lit up at the news.

"Mother! Mother! She didn't sleep at all!" he yelled at her, his smile becoming a little bit smug. Then he turned to me. "Congratulations! You get to marry me!" I think I stumbled at his news of getting to marry him.

"Um, sorry. Why would I do that? You're like 18? We just met."

Then, I realized I probably shouldn't have said that and clasped my hand over my mouth. "Hello? I want to leave! Help, help! Is anyone still there? Why won't anyone answer me?!" I called out into the now pitch black room.

Scared and afraid at what just happened my palms began to sweat. My breath was short and raspy and I wondered why I was so worried. This was all a dream, right?

"Hello?" I called out. No one answered. "Hello?" I called again. The entire experience reminding me of when I was eight and got trapped under a very large pile of snow. "Can anyone hear me? Can anyone see me? Can someone please wake me up!?!" There was no reply.

A cool breeze blew as I opened my eyes once more to see the white hospital room. It was bleak, white and cold, but the room left me feeling whole, like I wanted to be here, like I was supposed to be here! But, I didn't want that, right? I felt like I was losing a part of me, like something was wrong. I had been in this room my whole life, right? No windows, no people, no clock. Wait, no clock? That can't be right.

There was a little whimper from a curtain on the wall that hadn't been there when I had fallen asleep. "Who's there?" I called out. "Hello?"

"Hi," the curtain said in a small but powerful voice. "What is your name?" it asked.

"Ela, but my full name is Elizabeth."

"Oh," the curtain whimpered again almost disappointed and a little sad.

"Come out. I won't hurt you!"

"No!" it said firmly. "You're going to hate me!"

"Now hate is a strong word. Wow, I'm beginning to sound like my mother!" I turned to myself and smiled a bit.

A piercing scream filled the room and pounded through my head seeming to make me deaf. "STOP!!" I yelled. It stopped for a moment and a single lonely marble rolled out from under the curtain before the screech started again. "Stop! Please stop! I can't hear anything!"

The screaming stopped and the velvety purple curtain fell to reveal the small wooden box that used to be at the foot of my bed. I lifted myself out of my bed and onto the floor where I crawled towards the box, forgetting that I was supposed to be paralyzed and not able to walk.

"Oh, Ela! Are you okay? Did you fall out of bed?" Two firm and gentle hands scooped me up and brought me back to where I had started. I had never wanted Jack to leave so badly before. The anger that had reared up inside me when I first arrived at this horrid place made yet another appearance. "Ela, rest. I will get you the box." So he walked over to the small wooden box and placed it next to me.

I lifted off the lid to find a small journal. It was a deep red and had golden corner protectors on the covers. The spine had four golden rings along it. They were inside of bright red diamonds outlined with black. A blue sapphire gem cut to look like an imperfect heart created the clasp button on the page side of the journal. The cover was for the most part blank and looked like something should be added to it. This was something I would love, yet hate.

Chapter 9

Progress

*T*his journal is a very special one, one that will eventually save my life.

I did my best to open the journal and read the note inside. It said:

My Dearest Ela,

I give this journal to you with my love. Use it wisely and it will help you. I know it's hard for you to write, so this journal will write for you. Think it and it will be written. Stay safe. Remember I will always love you.

Love, Aunt Sophie.

I flipped the page and a single tear fell from my face onto the page of the journal, for Aunt Sophie had died a year ago. So how did she know I can't write? I flipped through the pages, and was at it for a while before I gave up. I closed it and thought, 'It is already July 2, 5934. So much time has passed since...'

"Ela, what is that? I just watched you flip through like 100 pages and you were nowhere *near* the end." I wanted to reply but I couldn't talk, not one bit. "Ela, are you okay?" Jack questioned, clearly not understanding that I couldn't talk! "Hey, Ela, can…" I didn't hear the last thing he said because I fell asleep, again.

I was no longer in that Princess and the Pea thing, but in a soft blue room with one light shining over a book in the center of it. There were two doors. One was labeled "Cure." The other said "Mask." Huh? It was a square room, and kind of reminded me of the cardboard box dream from earlier, only it was smaller, much smaller.

I walked over to the book lying on a brown pedestal and flipped to the first page. It had yellowing pages and sharp black letters reading:

> *If you are reading this then you have the disease, Nollremiabunt. There is only one cure: to dream. In fact you are in a dream right now, but that doesn't mean it isn't real. On the wall there are two doors. The one with the red sign saying "Cure" will lead you closer to the, well, cure. The other one with a green sign saying "Mask" will mask the disease so that it doesn't worsen and others will see you as "normal." Make your choice wisely, for every action you make has a consequence.*

I turned to the doors. I didn't know which one to choose, "Mask" or "Cure?" I chose the door on the left. It said "Cure." What is the worst thing that could happen? I thought. Famous last words.

Chapter 10

A Map

I opened the door and walked in. A warm surge passed through me as my physical appearance changed. I was no longer, um, how to say it, "messed up," but actually sort of cured! I was wearing jeans (I don't think I have ever worn jeans outside of my dreams!) and a plaid shirt. I was no longer tied down to that horrible hospital bed, or wearing a stiff hospital gown. It felt amazing!

I wasn't on that island anymore either, but in a beautiful green field. There was a river quietly flowing down the middle with one lonely tree by the river bank. I never wanted to leave. I turned and saw another book on another brown pedestal. I walked closer to it and opened it. A piece of paper fell out. I bent over and picked up the faded piece of paper that looked to be a part of a map. I stood back up to my full height of five feet.

When I went to look at the book I was sucked out of the dream and back into reality. In my hand I held the paper from my dream. I moved the paper up into the light. It shined through the thin piece of paper and onto my journal that was closed on my chest. It also caught a bit of the hand mirror on my chest and shined the light into my eyes. My diary lit up, glowing with a golden light that combined with the mirror nearly blinded me.

I tried to close my eyes to avoid it, but I couldn't manage to draw my eyes away. Before long the glowing lost a bit of its intensity and soon stopped. When it stopped the paper I was still holding became unbearably heavy, and because my arms were so weak from so little activity, it dropped, attaching itself to my journal. The cover seemed to become a jelly-like substance for just a second as a piece of paper came up and attached to the cover of my journal. A glow started at the seam of the two pieces of paper. It stopped leaving a partial map on the cover of my journal.

Chapter 11

Visiting the Past

I closely inspected the cover, looking at every detail. I placed my index finger over the map and set my finger on my home, for I recognized this as a map of Hoffoloff and San-fratta. I promptly fell asleep. I was in the blue room again and decided to go through the door marked "Cure." I found myself in the same outfit as before. I was in my own house where I was all better.

I walked into my room, a smile beginning to appear on my face. It was quickly wiped away when I saw myself on the phone, my eyes glossed over with water. The clock said it was 2:18 a.m. I saw the events of that terrible day when my mom was hit by that car and I was put in the hospital over again as though through someone else's eyes.

As I watched myself cry on my bed, I walked over to my black desk. I tried to open it. I don't know why, I just did. I lifted my hands up from the bottom of the lid, but they just went right through it. This happened to me four times. On the fifth try I got sucked out of the past like a bathtub draining water.

I woke up in the hospital gasping for air, glad that Jack had left. I knew I had to get home, but how? My legs felt

like mush. There was a knock on my door. It opened. Tanya
and Piper Emixer walked in, avoiding each other's glare.
Tanya and Piper have always been mad at each other, yet
no one knows why. I don't think they know why!

"Oh, Ela! Are you okay? You look terrible," Tanya said,
rushing to my side. Piper followed along and knelt down
closer to my head.

"Wow, way to be subtle. And really Tanya? No, she is not
alright. She's in the hospital," Piper stated, rolling her eyes.

"Hey Piper, there is no need to make me look stupid…
only to cover up how stupid you are!" Tanya shot back.

"Oh really now?" Piper began, turning on her heel and
rising to her full height as Tanya turned to face her. "I'm
the one covering up? Everyone can see that thick layer of
makeup you use to cover up your ugly face!" Piper walked
forward towards Tanya, poking her cheek.

I wanted to tell them to stop arguing, but the words
caught in my throat. Talking was almost entirely impossible
now with me being sick. Maybe I could learn sign language?
I waved at Tanya and Piper, catching their attention and
breaking their argument.

"Well, now we know she's awake, so Tanya, leave!" Piper
half shouted.

"If I didn't have to leave because of you, I would leave
anyway!" Tanya responded.

"What?" Piper asked and I thought.

"Yea, I didn't understand that either. Bye Ela! Piper." Tanya
gave her a cold glare as she walked out of the room slam-
ming the door.

"So, Ela, how have you been?" Piper knelt next to me
again, obviously unclear of what to say.

I rolled, or attempted to roll my eyes, but judging by
the look on her face, it didn't work. The door swung open
but I couldn't see who it was. Whoever this person was

frightened Piper because her eyes grew very large and she ran out of the now open door. I tried to roll my head to see who it was, but the effort was too much and I quickly fell asleep. Why does this keep on happening?!?

I don't think I dreamed. I honestly don't know what I did, but after dreaming for so long such really, really, really—well you get the point—weird dreams, it was even more weird not to dream. There was only black, a harsh black. Like that on a cloudy night with no moon nor stars, no wind nor sound, no people nor light. Just me in the never-ending dark. I think I was "floating." It was so hard to tell.

When my eyes fluttered open I was in a meadow filled with flowers. I had never seen such a beautiful place in person, only in a school book.

I did attend school for a few years, even though I am not very educated. It is not required on my island to attend school after you are fourteen.

I am sorry to say that when my parents… when my parents… when they…

"Ela!" That oh so familiar voice rang out. I was standing, so I knew I was either dreaming or—

"Flowers are water and fire is flowers! The ground is my locker and the sky is my food!" said Lillly.

I once went to summer camp with her where I learned to decipher her nonsense. Some say it is gibberish, but it is nothing of the sort.

"Ela!" I wheeled around to see Jack running up the side of the volcano towards me. I turned around to see my family standing behind Lillly.

"So, Ela, you gonna tell us what in the world that means?" I smiled at my brother, then opened my mouth, unsure as to whether I could talk or not.

"She said," I smiled at being 'normal' once more, "that my permanent cure lies on the island of Sanfratta, and I need to follow a map to find a flower to mix with one of these flowers." I gestured to the many flowers in the meadow.

"After the volcano erupts," I gulped and began wringing my hands a bit, worried about their reactions.

"Erupts! What does that mean? This volcano has been dormant for three-thousand years!" I always knew my mother was smart. I must take after my father...

"Well, it means exactly that. This volcano will erupt and the orchids will bloom into Fire-Orchids, a very rare type of orchid. I need to crush the two flowers together and I will have my cure." I looked around at the twelve eyes staring at me. Little did I know, but my life and the lives of all the people around me, would change. Some for the better, others for the worse.

Chapter 12

A Complicated Trip

"So, what are we waiting for? We need to catch the next ferry to Sanfratta and stay there until the volcano erupts. Easy, right?" Angela half asked, half stated. As she gets older I realize how bossy and obnoxious she is becoming, but at least she cares.

"Flies don't grow. Rivers can fly. Death can flower in the spring!"

"Um... what? I wish Lillly would just be quiet," Angela nagged.

"Really?" I asked, more to Lillly than anyone else. Lillly nodded. "Well, she says I have to go by myself using the last piece of the map in my room. The piece is on my desk." Now not only was everyone staring at me, except for Lillly, but their mouths were open in astonishment. Probably at the fact that I can understand Lillly.

"There's a map in your room?!?" Jack asked.

"Um... really? I just said that..." While Jack is amazing his IQ is a bit questionable.

"Anyway, when I get there I have to go to my house, then of course Sanfratta!"

I walked to the edge of the mountain and I looked back at my friends and family who were rooted to the ground.

This really is something I have to do all alone. Some sort of magic was keeping them in place. All I could hope for was for them to be safe.

I started down the volcano. When I was about halfway down I could feel my face start to slowly, very slowly, start to change back to its sickened state. Back to how it was when this started nearly a year ago. Night slowly turned into dawn as the sun began to rise. It was 2:30 a.m. People were coming out of their houses to start their day.

"Ela!" Tanya shouted from outside my house. I'm not sure why she was there. "Happy birthday!" It had slipped my mind, but could you blame me?

"Hi. Can I get into my house?" It looked like Tanya was going to move, but then she acted as if she hadn't heard me. I noticed my door was open just slightly.

"Ela! Your face!" While Tanya was and is my best friend she can be a bit, oblivious.

"Happy birthday El…" I turned around and saw my cousin Memna with her daughter Ally. They both looked at my face and screamed before hurrying away.

"Um, why did they scream?" Tanya asked, trying to secretly close the door.

I took a deep breath trying not to burst out at Tanya. "It's been almost a year of me being sick." I looked down at my feet, unable to meet her eyes. "You have gotten used to seeing me this way. Others are scared of me."

"Why?"

"Because no one can explain it! When someone is sick with some disease no one has ever heard of people worry. People fear. It is almost as though that is what is feeding my sickness. Magic doesn't exist, but then how do you explain me getting better and then this." I point to my face. "I'm scared. What if this disease kills me? What then? The only thing people can recognize is the paralysis. Now if you'll excuse me, I need to get into my house!" Tanya opened the door as she stepped aside.

I realized I had carelessly left the door unlocked when I went to the hospital a year ago. As I walked in, the unfamiliar smell of a stranger's house rushed forward to greet me. I wanted to run to my room, but I no longer knew the rules of the house. So I just walked to my room and to my desk.

Looking over at my bed, it still had my phone on it that I had dropped. The clock was flashing 4:52, so I knew the power must have gone out at some point. My bed was unmade and my pajamas were left lying on my floor. I lifted up the lid of my desk, but the only thing in there was my second grade report on the healing powers of Sanfratta. Then it hit me! The healing powers of Sanfratta! My one page report was the last part of the map. I sat down on my bed and a large puff of dust arose, making me sneeze repeatedly.

I pulled my diary out of my bag and set it on my lap. My foot was now tingling, and would soon go numb. The last time the map appeared on my journal, I had held the piece of paper up to the light, but the lights were off and the sun wasn't very high yet. I looked at my report and when my eyelids drooped I was carried away once more to the land of dreams.

Chapter 13

Inconvenient Dreaming

I opened my eyes to the soft blue room with the brown pedestal.

"You have got to be kidding me?!" I shouted out. Why couldn't I have any variety in my dreams?!

I walked over to the door marked "Cure." It was slightly stuck and I gave it a tug before it opened and I could walk through. I looked around at the deserted alley. The wind whistled by and I heard the sound of laughter.

"Who's there?" I asked into the alleyway. I was wearing a gray hoodie around my waist, but other than that, nothing had changed since my last dream when I was on the volcano.

"Jenna, look! A girl!" I turn around to see two little girls, one of whom looked very familiar.

"Who are you?" I asked, hoping to get a little bit more information, other than that of my gender.

"Well, I'm Lillly, spelled with three l's in the middle and this is Jenna!" Where was I? Lillly never spoke normally.

I opened my mouth to speak, but before I could, a girl whom I also recognized stepped through me. What?!

"I'm Sophie. I come from the island of Sanfratta. I am

looking for two young girls to be my apprentices. Would you like to be my apprentices?" She looked down at the two girls. Their eyes were so big and filled with wonder, it could do nothing but bring a smile to your face.

"Well… What would we be apprenticing in?" Jenna asked, pulling Lillly towards her and linking arms.

"We really should check with our parents first," Lillly added, a bit nervously.

"Well, magic of course! You have never heard of Sanfratta, have you?" She asked, a smile playing at the corners of her mouth.

"No, not really," Jenna responded, looking away, almost ashamed.

Sophie smirked at her like she was so much better than the two girls before her. The same thing that reared up inside me back in the hospital when I first learned my mom was okay, and when Jack had picked me up, made another appearance. I took a step forward and clenched my fist with a bit of the gray hoodie. I wanted to take those girls far, far away from her, take them home to their parents. If this is the same story Aunt Sophie had told me and my siblings about how she became the first person to travel outside of San Way Triangle, I never wanted to hear it again.

San Way Triangle is set apart from the rest of the world. The lone survivor of World War IV. The war on the mainland sent San Way Triangle out of reality and into the future where it could be safe, and the rest of the world back in time to try and fix its mistakes.

She had always made it seem like some wild adventure, making new friends, learning new things. I remember the cold and rainy nights Kris and I would spend with her, curled up by the fireplace, listening to her stories. It was those moments I wanted to stay in forever. It was those moments that made me feel like I belonged.

This scene before me put everything into place…. the two orphaned girls she met and took care of, even her clothes, almost entirely rags, and the green heart with a golden center that symbolized peace. She was the very image of a perfect citizen. These girls would do anything she asked.

"We should go…" Lillly said, pulling me out of my daze. I continued to watch the scene unfold before me. It was like something out of a virtual reality.

"No! I need two apprentices, and you two are… perfect!" She seemed to struggle as she finished her sentence.

"We need to evacuate the city!" The loud voice woke me up. I was hunched over my diary and I was still holding the piece of paper. "Ferries and all manner of boats will be taking passengers to Mannraway Island. There is no need to panic, but there is need to hurry. The Hoffoloff volcano will erupt soon and evacuation is VERY NECESSARY. There will be one more ferry leaving for Sanfratta in half an hour. If you have family living there you must go and warn them. Stick together. Scientists aren't sure when it will erupt." The woman's voice rang out, so clear it was like she was standing next to me.

I looked down at my diary again and noticed that I was no longer holding my report, but it had attached to my journal, leaving a full map of the islands creating the San Way Triangle. This is a place that is two-thousand years in the future from the mainland. That is why most people don't leave, unless you're my brother or aunt, the only people who have left the triangle and come back alive.

I shook my head in amazement before getting up and subconsciously wiping dust off my jeans. The door was still open, and as I walked outside there were people walking and running to the three main docks on the island. I headed for the one in the direction of Sanfratta. It took me about fifteen minutes to walk there as I was in a sort of daze. The world I knew was going to change. There was no stopping it.

I arrived at the dock where there were a handful of people. I made my way onto the large boat and took a seat near the window. I pulled out my diary and opened up to Aunt Sophie's note. Before I had time to react, the boat lurched beneath me, and we were off to Sanfratta.

"Not to alarm anyone, but the, ah, the volcano is beginning to erupt, smoke is rising and... Oh, wait, it seems there are six people on top of the volcano, they aren't moving, just frozen there."

"NOOOOOOOOO!" I screamed to the utter alarm of everyone there.

I looked out the window, and sure enough the volcano was starting to smoke and something was flying out of the mouth of it. It was a faint yellow bubble that rose carrying what appeared to be six people.

I gave a sigh of relief, sat back, and looked back down at my journal. I closed it and looked at the map. There was a moving red dot on it, heading from Hoffoloff to Sanfratta. That must have been me. The dot was following a blue dotted line and I guessed that was what I was supposed to follow. Talk about the classic treasure map.

The boat gave a lurch and it sped forward at top speed. "Buckle your seatbelts everyone. We have been slightly hit by the volcano that has now erupted. STAY SEATED!" he yelled. Lights began to flash inside of the boat and in that instance it felt more like I was on an airplane than on a boat.

Before I knew it, we were docking and I raced off, my journal in hand and many eyes staring at me with wonder and judgement. I didn't care though. I ran like I had never ran before. I ran through the town that had nearly been deserted. Everyone was fleeing to Mannraway Island, which is far away from Hoffoloff. I slowed down as I reached a freshwater pool. The map on my diary said that the flower was at the bottom of the pool.

I hadn't swam in so long, I didn't think at the time that my body would remember how. I looked through the clear water, and sure enough there it was. The violet-purple flower with a golden yellow center. I took off my shoes and socks and placed them at the edge of the water along with my sweater, bag, and journal. I rolled the cuffs of my jeans up a little bit as well. I pulled my hair up into a bun and walked into the welcoming waters.

I dove deeper, reaching nearer and nearer. My left foot then gave out to the oncoming paralysis. I could feel my lips changing and it became harder to keep the air in my mouth. I raced to the top of the water, breaking the surface and gasping for breath. Off in the distance I could just barely make out the erupting volcano. I needed to hurry, but how could I when I had fallen asleep?

Chapter 14

Dreams are the Key

The flower seemed so close, but I knew it was so far, in another reality even. I was just floating there in the water within my dream. A calm, peaceful feeling welled up inside of me. I could just stay here forever, I thought. But, no! I had to get that flower and become normal again. I didn't want it to take over!

"You can't keep going. You went through "Cure" too many times. You will die if you don't go back," a voice whispered eerily from the back of my head.

"No, it's so close. I, I can touch it!" I mentally whispered back, propelling myself towards the flower.

"Then face the consequences, Elizabeth. Remember those people who are on that erupting volcano for you. Remember the friend you pushed away, the one who had been paying your bills. Remember the being who brought you back to normal, the one who is saving your family and friend right now. Remember, they are all in this position because of you," the voice taunted. I wanted to give up, just go back. Maybe someone else could find the cure...

"NO!" I yelled out, losing my breath, but still going. "I don't know who you are, but I do know that I will NOT listen to you! You don't know them. You have never even met them."

"Oh, but yes I have. Why do you think you have come so close to the cure? Because of me!" the voice yelled back, pounding in my head, giving me a strong headache. "People are afraid of you, and I feed off of that fear. It makes me stronger, so much stronger. Your friend Tanya doesn't want to admit it, but she is the one who is the most afraid of you. That last encounter you had with her and Piper gave me enough energy to stay alive longer. Yes, I was the one who scared Piper away. I was the one in the corner at your little family reunion." The voice stopped talking and I pushed myself toward the flower.

"Give up Elizabeth. You can't win. I've always been one step ahead! With the diary, and taking Kris to Minnesota. You are no match for me!" The voice screamed from the back of my head. I yelled out in pain from the growing headache and realized something I was missing, the last piece.

"You know Sophia, I always liked you. You knew how to use people's emotions. I didn't realize though that you would come after me. Why? And why did you lie to Kris and me about your adventures? I know you did!" I again, mentally asked, trying to distract her. I didn't think I could really distract her, but it was worth a try.

"You were the smart one of the family, but that isn't saying much. Ah, what is sad though is how long it took you to figure this out. I don't blame you though. I am amazing," she sighed, making me shiver.

I was so close to the flower. Just one… more… push!

"I am only a wisp now of what I used to be. A great witch, training your brother to be the wizard he is. At one point I did teach Lillly and her little friend Jenna. Poor girls… such promise…" She almost seemed sincere, but I couldn't let that get in the way of what I wanted, what I needed!

"Magic doesn't exist!" I shouted out, getting a mouth full of water. I didn't care though, this was only a dream after all.

"Oh, Elizabeth, how ignorant you are. How else do you explain this?!? I trained Lillly, ugh, that was annoying, but how do you think you got your ability to understand her? FROM ME! I was always unappreciated. The middle child of five. Your mother was the baby and got the most attention. I was neglected. Too old to be cute, but too young to take care of myself. You are the same way. I thought you would help your poor old Aunt Sophie, whom you love so dearly!"

I almost wanted to go back and help her, but I couldn't. She had tricked me and like that book had said, every action has a cost, or something like that. "So, Sophia, you really think you are so wonderful? Well, I have the flower. All it will take is time before I am cured! Ha!" I mentally shouted at her, as I pulled the flower from the bottom of the lake. I was so exhausted and both legs were now paralyzed, but I knew it would pay off.

"Ah, time. Such a wonderful thing. A very powerful thing too. Why do you think your parents held onto that electric clock? Because it told the time. Time is the most important resource in our world. We are two-thousand years ahead of the rest of the world, so how do you think I survived my trips from here to Minnesota? Hmh? By harnessing TIME! Before that, let's just say it was a matter of guesswork, and the side effects sometimes resulted in, well, Lillly. Yes, it does help when trying to fake your own death. Honey, I'm here. I am in reality. You are not. You never really will be, for I control this time. I control all!" she laughed in the back of my head. I knew I needed to get to the surface of the water and wake up.

Chapter 15

A Cure

I put the stem of the flower in my teeth—hard to do when you only have one lip—and I propelled myself with my arms to the surface. My legs were just dead weight, completely paralyzed. I broke the surface and woke up, gasping for air, and reaching for my head in an attempt to subside the growing headache. The flower was still clenched in my teeth and sure enough there was Aunt Sophie standing at the water's edge, looking at me with slightly sad eyes. Her face was pale and she looked like she hadn't slept in, well, two-thousand years.

"How could you!?!" I screeched as I used my arms to crawl onto the sandy beach.

"How could I not? I needed to become more than a wisp, so I used you to generate fear. I need more, but I guess I will have to wait on that." She looked at me as if it were my fault. I guess somehow in a very twisted way it was.

My hair fell in front of my face and I saw it was white. Soon it was hard for me to breathe as my nose collapsed, along with my arms. I lay there on the beach next to my things, Aunt Sophie close by.

"I had such high hopes for you, but I will have to go elsewhere. Don't think of calling for help. This tiny island is deserted. I don't see why anyone would want to live here. It's so small."

"It's beautiful," I croaked.

"Oh, you poor thing. Have fun here." With that, she floated up into the sky before disappearing all together.

"What a witch!" I whispered angrily to myself.

With nothing else to do, I reached for my diary. I didn't care that Aunt Sophie had given it to me. I was going to write in it, write what had happened. I opened it up to the first page and began my entry.

Dear Diary,

My life recently has been really tough. I never thought this would happen, but it did. I have found a cure, and I am hoping someone will return for me on this island, but that might never happen. Listen closely dear reader... this is my story.

Healing Powers of Sanfratta

By Ela Rose

S anfratta is one of the three islands in the San Way Triangle. Sanfratta has healing powers. This report is about those healing powers.

Sanfratta has very exotic wildlife that ends up giving us the cure to many things. For example, cancer. The wild blueberries on Sanfratta can cure any type of cancer!

Sanfratta has rain different from ours. It rains magic! Seriously! The atmosphere is different in that one place, giving it a healing effect that will create just about any type of cure, for any type of disease.

Sanfratta isn't a big island, like Mannraway, but it is beautiful. Here is a list of plants and animals that have been known to cure diseases, thought two-thousand years ago to be incurable.

Polio... The flowers at the bottom of Lake Willa cure the paralysis, and the purple vines, when boiled in Sanfratta rain, will wash the disease out of your system.

Asthma... Is simply cured by having a pet mini tiger.

Pain in general... Cured with treatment of a paste from the golden bananas, shavings from a rhino's horn that has died of natural causes, and water from Lake Willa.

The Common Cold... This one is a more recent discovery, but it has been proven to work. Strawberries and raspberries boiled down to a liquid mixed with a leaf from a palm tree and a strand of the patient's hair. Each mixture is unique to the patient because no two common colds are the same.

SIGMA'S BOOKSHELF

Sigma's Bookshelf (www.SigmasBookshelf.com) is an independent book publishing company that exclusively publishes the work of teenage authors, who are between the ages of 13 - 19. The company was founded in 2016 by Minnesota teenager Justin M. Anderson, whose first book, *Saving Stripes: A Kitty's Story*, was published when he was 14, and has since sold hundreds of copies.

"I know there are a lot of other teenagers out there who are good writers and deserve to have their work published, but don't have access to the kinds of resources I do. I wanted to help them," he said.

Sigma's Bookshelf is a sponsored project of Springboard for the Arts, a nonprofit arts service organization. Contributions on behalf of Sigma's Bookshelf may be made payable to Springboard for the Arts and are tax deductible to the extent permitted by law. Donations can be made online at www.SigmasBookshelf.com/donate, and will help cover the expenses associated with bringing teenagers' books to market at no cost to them.

www.ingramcontent.com/pod-product-compliance
Lightning Source LLC
Chambersburg PA
CBHW020624120726
47905CB00003B/929